ELMER
and SUPER EL

David McKee

Andersen Press

Elmer, the patchwork elephant, was taking his morning walk when he heard an "Oh no!" Looking round, he spotted a small elephant dressed in an outfit that he recognized. "Hello, Super El," Elmer said with a smile. "What's the problem?"

"Look," said the small elephant, showing his torn outfit. "That thorn bush attacked me! If I'm seen like this, I'll be laughed at. That's not very super."

"Aunt Zelda will soon fix that," said Elmer. "We'll just have to make sure that you're not seen. Our first problem will be to pass the elephants. I'll distract them. Come on. It will be fun!"

Elmer went to the elephants and called out,
"I've just heard a good joke, listen."
The elephants all looked at him.
"There was an elephant, a lion and a fish . . ."
he began. "Oh dear, I've forgotten the rest!"
"That's a good one," the elephants laughed.
"Elephants never forget!"
Meanwhile Super El slipped past unnoticed.

Elmer and Super El hadn't gone far when they heard Lion and Tiger approaching. "Hello," said Elmer. "Nice day for it."

"Eh? What?" asked Lion and Tiger together.
They were confused enough not to notice the little elephant
on the rocks above them.

"We're near the hippos," said Elmer. He picked up a broken bush. "Hide behind this."

"Taking a bush for a walk, Elmer?" chuckled a hippo.

"There's an elephant behind it," Elmer replied.

"Always joking, Elmer," the hippos laughed. Once they were safely past, Elmer said, "Wait here, Super El. I've an idea how we can get past both Snake and the rabbits."

The rabbits were listening enthralled to
Snake, as the two elephants slipped past them.
"What's going on?" asked Super El.
"I asked Snake to tell the rabbits about the time he
tricked me and the elephants," said Elmer. "He tells
it beautifully. They haven't noticed us."

When they came to the crocodiles, Elmer threw a branch into the river to distract them. Then he and Super El crossed in the confusion that followed.

"It's not going to be easy to pass the monkeys," said Elmer. "Leave that to us," said the birds.

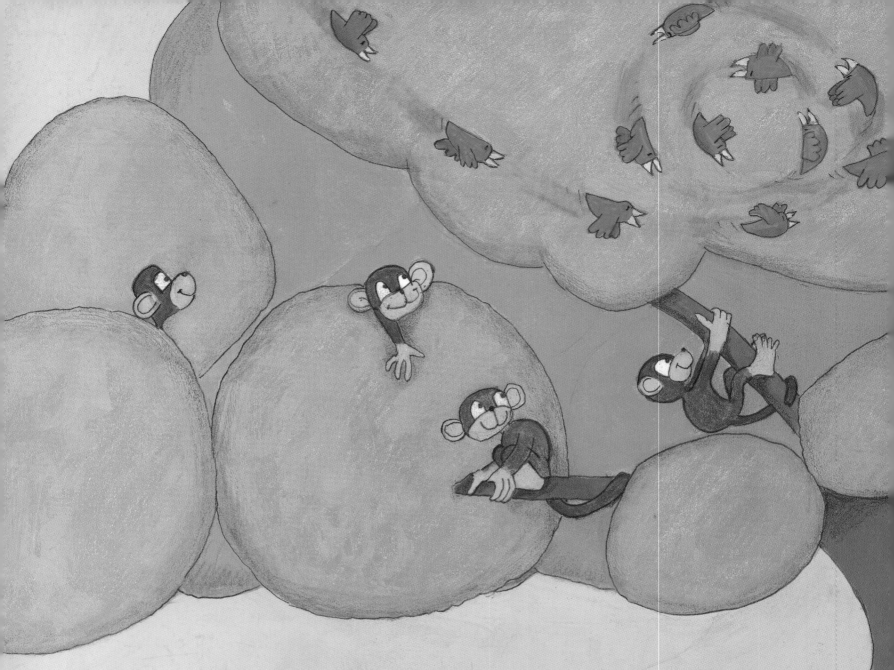

The birds were wonderful. They sang and flew in patterns above the monkeys' heads. The monkeys were too fascinated to notice the elephants. The little elephant nearly stopped to watch, but Elmer pushed him along.

"Thanks, birds," said Elmer later. "You were
fantastic! Look, there's Aunt Zelda saying goodbye
to some friends. As soon as they've left, we'll go to her.
Remember, she doesn't always hear too well."

When the others had gone, Elmer said, "Hello, Aunt Zelda, this is my friend Super El."
"Yes, I'm very well, thank you, Elmer dear," said Aunt Zelda. "But your friend's suit looks in a bit of a state. Shall I mend it?"
"Oh, yes please!" said the little elephant.

Elmer lay down and watched as Aunt Zelda set to work with a thread so fine you could hardly see it.

"Aunt Zelda," said Elmer, "you are a wonder."
"Thunder, dear? I didn't hear anything," said
Aunt Zelda.
Super El smiled, and Aunt Zelda quickly
finished the repairs.

"Thank you, now I feel super again," said the little elephant. "I think you're both wonderful. Maybe one day I can do something for you."
With that, he shot off like a rocket into the sky.
He looped back just once to wave goodbye.
"If he's going to rush about like that he'll spoil his clothes again," said Aunt Zelda.
"Probably," said Elmer, chuckling. "Probably."

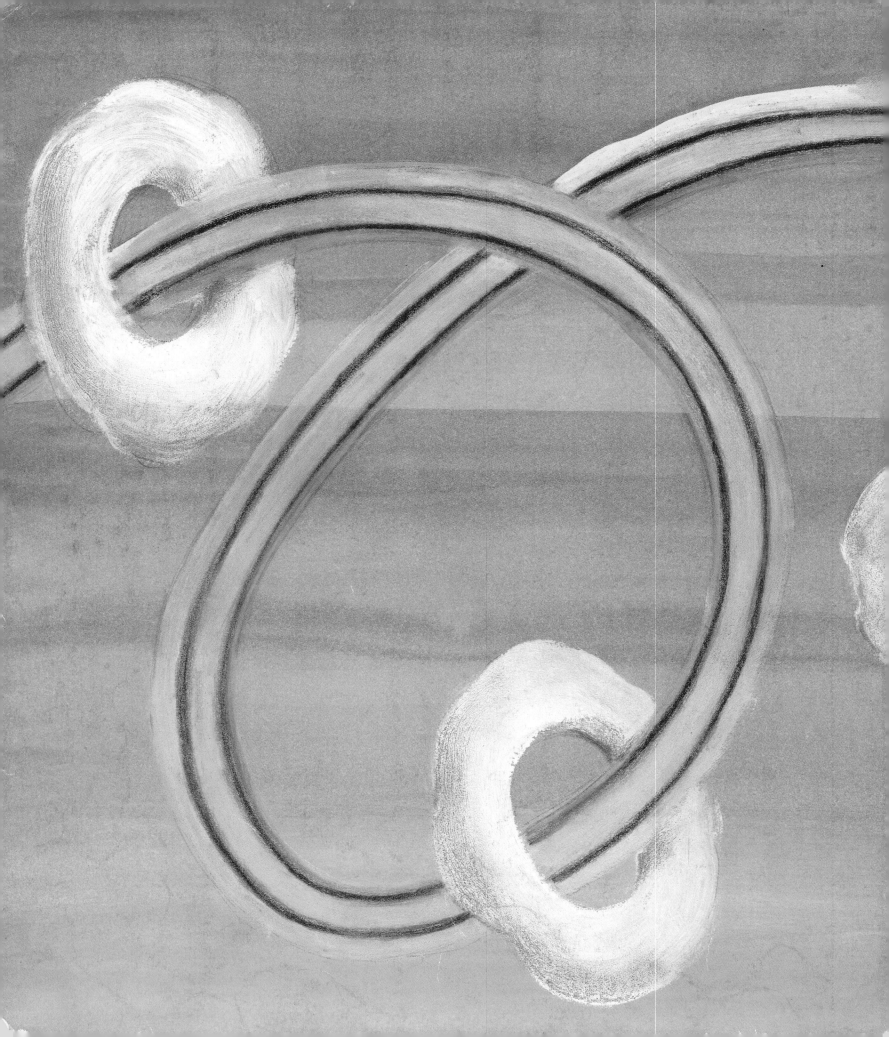

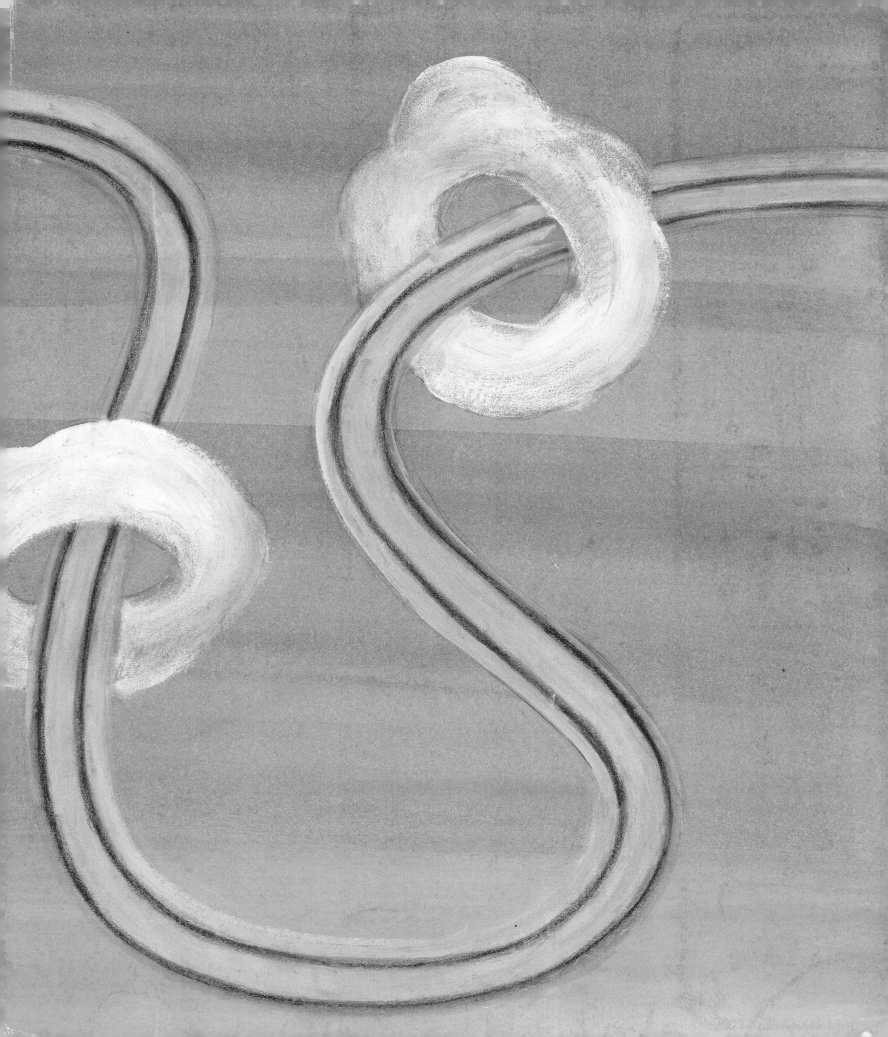

Read more ELMER stories

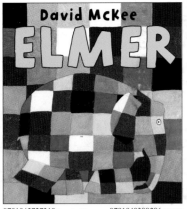

9781842707319 (paperback)   9781849399296 (eBook)
Also available as a book and CD

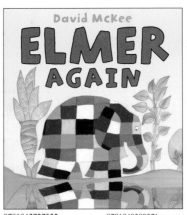

9781842707500 (paperback)   9781849399371 (eBook)
Also available as a book and CD

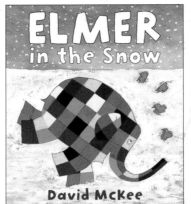

9781842707838 (paperback)   9781849399418 (eBook)
Also available as a book and CD

9781842709504 (paperback)   9781849399388 (eBook)
Also available as a book and CD

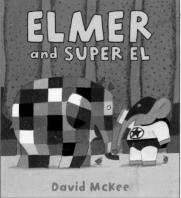

9781842707401 (paperback)

9781842708385 (paperback)   9781849399401 (eBook)

9781842707739 (paperback)   9781849399432 (eBook)

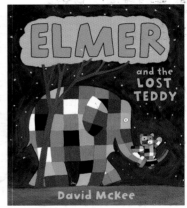

9781842707494 (paperback)

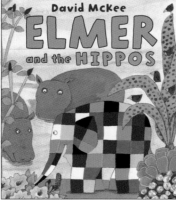

9781849394574 (paperback)   9781849399289 (eBook)

9781842709818 (paperback)   9781849399500 (eBook)

9781842708392 (paperback)   9781849399449 (eBook)

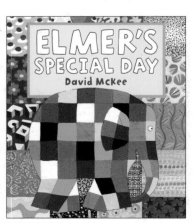

9781842709856 (paperback)

Elmer titles are also available as Apps.

Find out more about David McKee and Elmer, visit:

www.andersenpress.co.uk